My "r" Book

(Blends are included in this book.)

Little 

had a 

"I will fill my box," he said.

Little  found rabbits

and radishes.

He put them into his box.

Little 

found a  rooster.

"In you go,
rooster," he said.

He found a raccoon.

The raccoon ran.

Little r ran after him and...

put him into

the box.

Then he saw a rat.

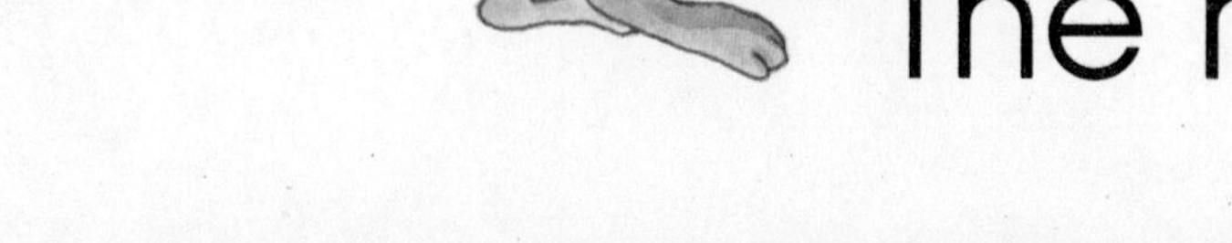

The rat ran.

Little caught the rat.

Guess
where he put the rat?
Then he ran down the road.

Little r found
a reindeer

and a rowboat.

He put all his things into the rowboat.

Away he went.

It began to rain.

So he put on his raincoat.

Then he found a rhinoceros

and a raft.

So he put all his things

on the raft.

But the raft ran into a rock.

The reindeer fell off the raft.

Little

found a rope.

He pulled the reindeer
back onto the raft.

"Let's rest," he said.

They rested under a rainbow.

Then the rabbits said,

"Let's run a race."

They ran up the road to...

a rose bush,

Little said,

"Let's play
'Ring-Around
the-Roses'."

And they did.

rat
reindeer
hinoceros
roses
raccoon
rabbits
rooster

More words with Little r.

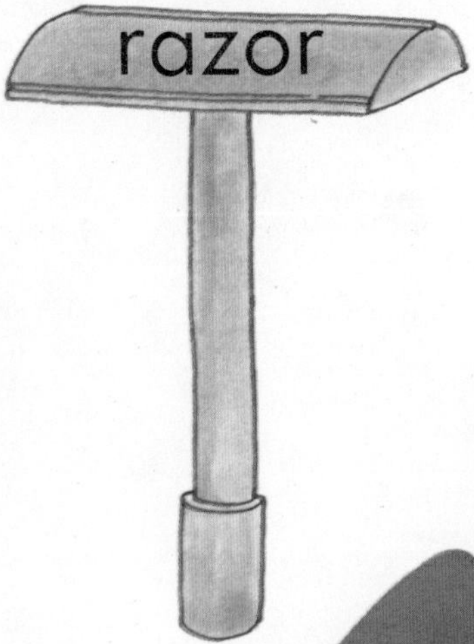

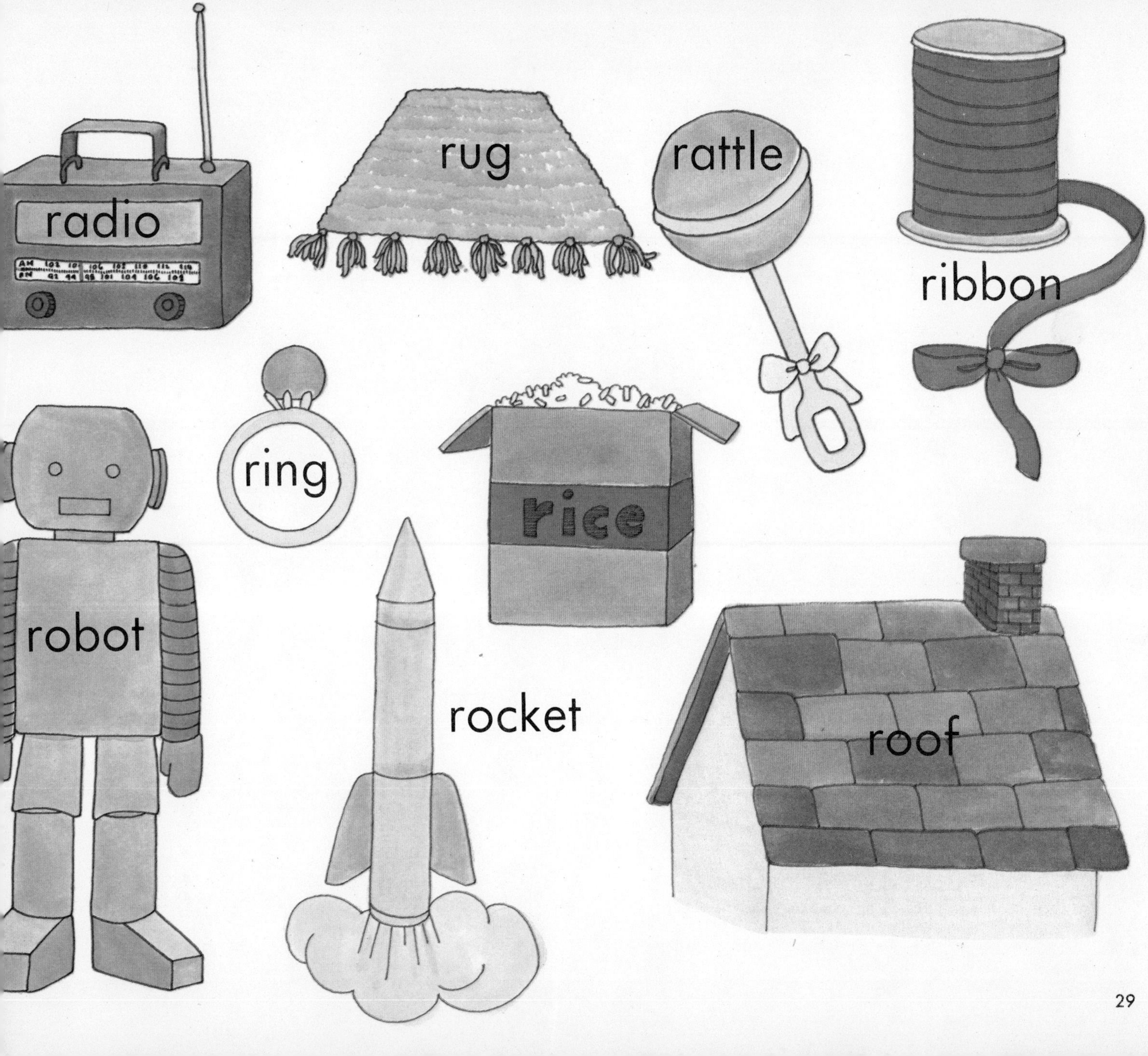
radio
rug
rattle
ribbon
ring
rice
robot
rocket
roof